The H

60-Minute Psycho-Thriller

D / T / N

CHAPTER 1

I lift my head and see the endless row of barren walls illuminated by cold, harsh light. The light seems to come from thin strips embedded in the ceiling. My head is throbbing. I don't know how I got here. Everything seems unreal, as if reality has frozen around me. I feel a slight pressure in my chest, a vague fear. I have no sense of direction.

No clues as to time or place. My clothes are simple: an inconspicuous T-shirt, dark trousers. Nothing indicates that I am following a specific purpose or striving towards a goal. Just this corridor, as sterile as a hospital ward, only without life, without human noises.

Behind me, a heavy metal door protrudes from the wall, angular and gray. I press my hand against the cold metal. The handle doesn't move a millimeter. A locked door, as if I were denied any way back. For a moment, I toy with the idea of banging on the door and calling for help. But the silence seems impenetrable and swallows up any sound before it can take shape.

I carefully take a step forward. Each step echoes eerily in the corridor, as if my own movements were accusing me. The floor beneath my shoes seems to be made of a smooth material. My breathing is shallow and I can feel the sweat running down the back of my neck. I don't know how far this corridor stretches. I can't see the end. The bright lights stretch into the distance, without interruption.

»Hello?« I ask into the emptiness and flinch at my own voice. It sounds rough and strange in the absolute silence. »Is anyone there?« No one answers. Silence. Not even an echo. I swallow hard and run my hand over my forehead. The cold of the hallway reaches my bones. Or is it just my insecurity that intensifies this chill inside me?

I continue on my way with difficulty. I feel the impulse to walk faster, but at the same time I'm afraid of reaching the end of the corridor too quickly. Perhaps there is something hidden there that I don't want to see. My feeling of loneliness intensifies with every step. There are no signs of a way out, no markings on the walls, no doors. Just endless white, an electric hum, and my heart pounding in my chest.

I stop and take a deep breath. Maybe there's a trick to the locked door after all, maybe I've just touched the wrong place. But the thought of a hopeless way back chokes my throat. I guess I have no choice but to keep going and look for answers at an unknown destination. A single question forms in my mind: who brought me here, and why?

I involuntarily touch my arms, my shoulders, my neck. I search for scratches, puncture marks, anything that might reveal what has been done to me. Nothing. It seems as if I am unharmed. Nevertheless, my insides feel unsettled, as if on the verge of an unpredictable storm. I swallow again, the taste in my mouth is dry and bitter.

I walk on, my footsteps fading into this corridor-like nothingness. The walls seem alienated, angular, constantly flickering in the glare of the strips embedded in the ceiling. Every shadow attracts my attention, although I can barely make out anything. Just this blinding white, without interruption. I keep looking over my shoulder, even though I know that the closed metal door behind me won't allow me to turn back.

Sometimes I imagine I see someone or something, but when I take a closer look, there is only emptiness. The uncertainty screams inside me louder than any real danger could. My breathing is intermittent, the air tastes of metal.

Suddenly I hear a strange scratching sound, as if something is grazing the wall. I pause, my muscles tense, and listen. But the next second, everything is dead silent again. My pulse races. I force myself to keep going because the hope of a solution drives me on. There must be a passage somewhere here, an exit, another door. This corridor can't be everything.

Every step echoes eerily. The uniform panels on the ceiling and side walls rob me of any sense of space. Without a cell phone or watch, I lose all sense of time.

I call out again: »Is anyone here?« No answer, just a fleeting echo. An oppressive buzzing remains as a constant companion, like the heartbeat of this endless corridor. I feel the urge to run, but can't bring myself to do so. The fear of reaching the end and finding something terrible there is too strong. But the possibility of being trapped in this barren corridor forever is also unbearable.

Suddenly, the light flickers and my breath catches. There is darkness for a moment. My heart threatens to burst until the lights come on again. There is no rescue in sight, just the eternal white infinity and a floor whose surface seems slippery with every step. I breathe in and out deeply, trying to calm my nerves.

My throat is dry, my stomach empty. How long have I been walking around here? I have no answer. The wall feels smooth and cold as I my fingertips over it. Not a hidden crack anywhere, no switch, nothing. This place seems perfectly sealed, as if someone had created it specifically to isolate me.

Another breeze brushes my face. Light, but noticeable. I decide to walk in the direction it's coming from. Each step brings me closer to a possible door or a gap through which the air is seeping.

The corridor seems endless. I lose myself in monotonous thoughts until a new scratching noise snaps me out of my stupor. This time it sounds closer, as if something is driving right next to me. I turn around hastily and press myself against the wall. But there is no one there. My throat tightens and my legs tremble. Am I imagining everything? This place is playing with my mind. I have to keep going. I can't stand still.

CHAPTER 2

My knees are weak, my heart beats hard against my chest. I feel the back of my neck, trying to calm myself down. All I can hear is the buzzing of the ceiling lights. The silence is driving me mad.

Then I hear something that sounds like distant footsteps, soft and muffled. I feel a cold shiver run down my spine. I turn around quickly, but nothing moves. No figure, no shadow. Just these relentlessly bright walls. The feeling of being watched intensifies. I don't see any cameras or mirrors anywhere. But it's as if eyes are glued to every pore of my skin.

I quicken my steps in an effort to escape this invisible gaze. But with every step, my fear echoes louder. The light flickers briefly and I imagine I see a shadow where none can be. My breathing is intermittent. Something is lurking in these sterile white walls without showing itself.

After a few meters, I spot a darker spot on the wall to the right. I rub my eyes to see it better. Sure enough: a scratched sketch or doodle, barely bigger than the palm of my hand. It looks hastily carved into the surface. My throat constricts as I try to interpret the line. »A map?« I whisper. An arrangement of lines, arrows and symbols. They could indicate corridors or rooms.

My pulse continues to accelerate. Who left this mark and why? I lean closer, run my fingers over the carved grooves. A triangle, a circle, tiny dots. Lines intersect between them as if it were a complicated plan. One arrow points to the left, one to the front. How fitting, I think bitterly, as the whole thing here could be a single labyrinth.

Suddenly that unsettling feeling comes over me again. I drive around. Nothing. Just this bright white staring back at me. I swallow, my mouth is dry. »There's no one there,« I tell myself, but a part of me doesn't believe it. Something like an invisible presence pervades the hallway. The sterile air is filled with my racing heartbeat.

I return to the map and try to memorize every detail. It seems to show that there is a side path somewhere. However, I can't see any turn-off. The walls seem smooth and unbroken. Perhaps there is a hidden door. Or this scrawl is just a cry for help from another person who was trapped here. I wonder if she has managed to find a way out. The humming above me changes its tone for a moment, as if it has heard my questions.

I run my hand along the wall, letting it glide over the cold material. There is no handle here, no gap. But on the map, a line runs along the side of the main corridor. My stomach tightens. I try to trace the route with my finger.

I pause as I hear a scratching sound, much closer this time. I look in the direction from which the sound came. The ceiling lights flicker and the darkness flashes for the blink of an eye. My pulse races, but there's no one there. Is it just a trick on my hearing? Or are there secret doors hidden here, through which others scurry silently?

I realize that I keep turning around, expecting to catch sight of something that only gives birth to my fear. I try to calm myself down, breathing in and out deeply. My gaze falls on the carved map again. Maybe it's the only thing that can lead me out of here. I should memorize these structures. I tap the enigmatic triangle with my finger, touch the strange square that lies off to the side. I wonder if there is a mechanism that can be connected to it.

A loud cracking sound hits my bones. I flinch violently and stop abruptly. The footsteps echo again, this time irregularly, as if someone is scurrying away. Wet fear creeps into my blood. I press myself against the wall, staring into the glaring distance. »Hello?« I whisper. Nothing. No echo, just my fear echoing in my head. My legs tremble.

Despite my growing unease, I force myself to go ahead. There must be a clue somewhere that matches the map. I run my hand over the wall, trying different places. No handle, no crack. The corridor continues to show its most sterile side. The surroundings seem designed to confuse people.

I change direction and take a few steps back, always careful not to lose sight of the carved sketch. If I get too far away, I end up losing my only possible orientation. But standing around doesn't get me anywhere either. The light flickers again.

Suddenly, footsteps again. This time they literally thunder in the distance, seeming hurried and threatening. »Who's there?« I call out, a little louder. No answer, just a quiet fading of the sounds. I feel goose bumps on my arms and feel over the scribble again. Whoever left it could have experienced a similar horror. An image emerges in my mind of desperate fingers digging into the wall to sketch a map before every shred of hope is extinguished.

I close my eyes briefly and try to memorize the order of the symbols. Then I force myself to move on. My footsteps echo in this hall of silence. The corridor doesn't change, remains infinite and cool. I lose track of time and have no idea how long I've been here. Everything seems to become one: the light, the wall, my fear.

Once again, I hear a scratching sound very close to me. I duck down and hold my breath. I expect to see a strange silhouette at any moment. But the buzzing of the lamps remains my only companion. It is unclear whether someone is deliberately trying to drive me mad. My body is kept awake by adrenaline. My senses are playing tricks on me, or something really is lurking around here.

CHAPTER 3

I continued on my way. In the distance, I heard a quiet sobbing that sounded like an echo. I stopped abruptly and listened intently.

Suddenly I noticed a small movement on the floor. A child was sitting in a barely lit corner of the corridor. It was no more than seven or eight years old, dressed in dirty clothes and with pale, expressionless eyes. The child sat on the cold floor with his eyes downcast, not looking at me. My heart pounded violently and my breath caught. I slowly stepped closer

»You're too late,« the child whispered in a voice that was barely more than a breath. The words penetrated my ears like a frosty wind and sent a shiver down my spine. I stood still, unable to grasp the situation. My mind raced as I stared into the pale eyes that refused to look.

I took a step forward to get closer to the child when I suddenly realized that it had disappeared. Where a few seconds ago the child had been sitting on the cold floor, there was now only an empty spot. I knelt down and looked for signs of his existence in the dim light. All I could see was the cold glow of the sterile white hallway. My heart beat faster and an oppressive feeling spread through me. Had I imagined everything? Or was this another sinister clue in this inscrutable place?

Confused, I stood up and turned to the wall where I had previously discovered the scribble. With shaky fingers, I stroked the cold surface to get my bearings. On the smooth, immaculate wall was written clearly: »Time is different in here.«

I took a step back and looked at the message. The statement was unmistakable, but at the same time puzzling. What did it mean that »time is different"? The words seemed to be projected into the sterile room, as if they were trying to convey to me a secret knowledge that lay hidden in the shadows of this building. The memory of the whispering child and his haunting words mingled with the sight of the childish writing, and my mind struggled to form a clear thought. There were no other clues to help me decipher the meaning.

With trembling hands, I pressed the wall where the childish writing had been and tried to memorize every detail. The letters were not randomly placed, but seemed almost like a clue to something hidden. My eyes searched the rest of the hallway as if they could find more signs there.

The silence around me became more oppressive and every breath seemed to increase the tension. I could feel the cold sweat on my forehead as I stepped back to the spot where the child had been sitting. I raised my eyes, expecting to see him again, but the spot remained empty. The words »You're too late« echoed in my head and I felt an icy grip tighten around my heart.

A brief gust of wind – or perhaps just a figment of my imagination – caused the ceiling lights to flicker for a moment. For a tiny moment, it seemed as if time had changed, as if the rhythm of the room had slowed down. But then the usual brightness returned and the corridor remained unchanged. I could only stand still and look at the scrawled message, which still seemed to make me understand that this was no ordinary place.

With every step, a sense of inescapable destiny entered me, although I didn't understand what it meant. The corridor was a labyrinth of cold light and shadow in which every memory silently revealed itself. Time seemed to stretch as if the rules didn't apply. I had to keep walking, even if every step brought me closer to the unknown. Every breath was heavy and the darkness pressed relentlessly on my chest.

CHAPTER 4

At that moment, I felt dark memories of times gone by stirring in my mind. Fleeting images from my childhood seemed to manifest themselves in the corners of the hallway, as if the wall wanted to reveal the forgotten moments.

A faint image emerged: I saw the small garden in front of my parents' house where I used to play. The old swing swung softly in the wind and my parents' laughter mingled with the sound of the falling leaves. A cold shiver ran down my spine as I realized how foreign this place was and at the same time so close to my heart. The memories were fleeting, almost like mirages, and they faded as soon as I focused on my path. Nevertheless, there was a silent pain in these images, a memory of lost light-heartedness and the loneliness that now surrounded me.

I walked on, my steps uncertain and hesitant. Suddenly my eyes fell on a door that appeared in the sterile wall. Its appearance made me freeze: it involuntarily reminded me of the front door of my parents' house. The worn wood, the slightly faded colors and the narrow handle, which seemed so familiar to me, made the door seem alive. I approached the door with trembling hands, but when I touched the handle, I felt that it was locked. There was no latch to open the way and the familiar structure remained inaccessible. An uneasy feeling spread through me, as if the memory itself was showing me a boundary that could not be overcome.

My thoughts circled as I looked at the closed front door. It was like a symbol of everything I had lost – the familiar sounds, the warm smells, the home light – now all these things were just faded shadows. Instead, all that greeted me was the cold, clinical silence of this place. I stroked the unyielding surface with my fingertips, as if trying to find a spark of warmth or memory, but all that remained was the rough feeling of metal and stone. There was no way in, no way out, and the pain of memory mingled with the oppressive fear of the unknown.

With a heavy heart, I turned back to the path. The hallway seemed to lengthen relentlessly, and every corner bore the veil of times past. The shadows of memory were overlaid by the barren walls, and I felt my past and present unite in an ominous dance. As I walked on, I suddenly noticed something that made my breath catch. A mirror, half concealed in an alcove, reflected the flickering light in ghostly patterns. As I stepped closer, I stared into the glass and recognized – almost unbelievably – my own reflection. But it was not the image I had expected.

The reflection showed me, but older. My face was marked by lines and shadows that I had never seen before. The eyes staring back at me from the mirror looked tired and filled with a deep sadness. I couldn't tell if it was a harbinger or just a coincidence in this labyrinth of light and darkness. »Who are you?« I whispered, as if I wanted to elicit a voice from the reflection. But it didn't answer. Instead, the apparition remained a silent, unsettling presence. This encounter made me tremble, as if I was looking into the future and losing a part of myself at the same time.

I took a step back and the reflection remained firmly in place, as if it were a silent witness to all my futile efforts to escape the hallway. The ominous apparition in the glass made me wonder if I hadn't become a prisoner in this place myself. The memory of my lost childhood, the familiar front door that remained locked, and now this reflection – all of this combined to form an impenetrable web of fear and uncertainty. Every step forward seemed to be a step into my own past, which I couldn't shake off.

As I walked on, the shadowy memories forced themselves back into my consciousness. A quick glance in the mirror gave me a glimpse of another moment: a sunny afternoon, the laughter of friends and innocent play in the dust. But these images were imbued with a deceptive lightness that stood in stark contrast to the oppressive darkness that now surrounded me. The memories passed as quickly as they had come, but left a lasting impression of loss and despair. I tried to concentrate on the path, but the past intruded more and more with every step.

The mirror, which showed me older, remained in my field of vision and seemed to reveal more to me than I understood. The lines on my face looked like signs of a lived time, as if every wrinkle told a story that I had long forgotten. The familiar expression seemed to dissolve and there was an air of eeriness in this altered appearance that took my breath away. The connection between the image in the mirror and the fleeting memories of my childhood seemed to fade, while the present revealed itself in a dark symphony of light and shadow.

A cold shiver ran through my body and my heart beat faster, as if it could sense the impending change. At that moment, the boundaries between past and present blurred. The eerie presence in the mirror seemed to be a warning to me, a silent reminder that in this labyrinth I not only had to walk the corridor, but also the shadows of my own history. Every crease in the reflection seemed like an echo of days gone by, and I could almost hear the sound of children's voices laughing softly in the darkness.

I took a step back and let my gaze wander across the corridor. The flickering light painted ghostly patterns on the walls and the silence seemed to capture my every breath. With trembling hands, I clenched my fist as I looked at the mirror again. There was a quiet desperation in the eyes of my older version that fascinated and terrified me at the same time. It was as if I saw the traces of a future that would be inevitable and painful. The thought of it made me pause for a moment as I tried in vain to find my way back.

I turned back to the corridor, but the path seemed even more confused now. The familiar shadows of memory mingled with the ominous present, and every step felt like an advance into an abyss. Without a word, I stepped into the corridor that led on. The faint light accompanied me, and every shadow revealed something familiar and unknown at the same time. The walls offered no further clues, and I knew I had to accept the uncertainty myself.

Suddenly I heard a soft noise again, barely more than a whisper, mingling with the murmur of my thoughts. I paused and listened. It seemed as if the silence opened up and revealed a secret sound to me. There was something unspoken in this sound, a hint that could not be put into words. For a brief moment, I felt the shadows of memory stirring in my mind again, and I saw the garden, the swing and the laughter – so fleeting that it almost seemed like a dream.

I forced myself to lift my eyes and step into the corridor that led on. Every step was a battle against the deceptive security of the past. The closed door and the mirror image that showed me my changed self accompanied me incessantly. Its presence was relentless, a constant reminder that there was no way back. So I walked on, with a heavy heart and the knowledge that every memory preserved a part of me in this eerie labyrinth.

As I entered a narrower passage, I stopped abruptly. A single sentence was emblazoned on the wall in front of me in childish handwriting, carved into the cool surface: »Time is different in here.« The words were shocking in their simplicity, as if they questioned the reality of the place. For a moment, it seemed as if time paused to convey this message to me. But before I could think about it any further, I turned back to the corridor.

I had barely taken a step when, in a fleeting moment, I suddenly caught another glimpse in a mirror mounted in a side alcove. There I stood – older, marked by the years and the countless steps in this merciless hallway. The reflection revealed a face that was both strange and painfully familiar, eyes heavy with untold stories. I could not avert my gaze as the silence surrounded me and my heart pounded in the darkness.

I turned away, my eyes fixed on the endless hallway, and took a hesitant step forward. But when I looked at the mirror again, my heart seemed to stop for a moment before everything ended abruptly and my world quietly shattered.

CHAPTER 5

I had barely taken another step when I discovered a door on a side wall that was different from the others. Its solid wood, which bore witness to a slight sheen of times gone by. With a trembling hand, I approached the door, which seemed as if it could reveal more than just another room in this relentless labyrinth.

Behind the door, which opened with a soft squeak, stood a figure that took my breath away. There stood a doppelganger of me – outwardly identical in every detail, but her gaze was blank and expressionless. Her eyes, which usually sparkled with life, seemed to stare into nothingness, as if they were being crushed by an invisible weight. For a moment, time stood still and I could hardly believe what I was seeing.

I stepped closer, fascinated and at the same time frightened by the uncanny resemblance. The doppelganger remained motionless, as if she wanted to confront me in a silent mirror of my own existence. Her features were flawless, every line of my face could be found in her, but there was no expression to indicate emotion. It was as if I was standing in front of a faceless image that showed me the distance between reality and illusion.

»Who are you?« I dared to ask, my voice barely more than a whisper in the oppressive silence of the hallway. The doppelganger slowly raised her head, and her vacant gaze seemed to want to penetrate me. Without a single sign of hesitation, she began to speak as if every question she asked was part of a strictly rehearsed test. Her voice sounded soft and eerie at the same time.

»Do you remember the day it all began?« she asked in a tone that was both demanding and indifferent. Her words hung in the air and I felt a lump forming in my throat. The question seemed to penetrate the depths of my memory, as if it wanted to mercilessly reveal all the hidden secrets of my past.

My thoughts raced. In this place, memories were too real, as if they were part of the fabric of this eerie labyrinth. But before I could answer, the doppelganger continued: »What did you lose when you left the path?«. Her questions caught me off guard and I felt like I was trapped in a game where every answer would determine the next step. It was as if this encounter was not accidental, but purposefully orchestrated – a test of my identity, my past and my destiny.

I tried to form a clear thought as the words settled in my mind. Every sentence from the doppelganger acted like a mirror, showing me hidden sides of myself. Her questions drilled into my memory, evoking images that I thought I had long forgotten. The pain of past losses, the unresolved fears and the quiet doubts about my path – all of this mingled with the eerie silence of the hallway.

»Do you remember losing your smile?« she continued, and her voice sounded almost melancholy, as if she were speaking a truth that was too deep inside me to ignore. I felt my palms feel damp and a cold sweat broke out. The question hit me unexpectedly and opened up old wounds that I had long tried to hide. I wanted to answer, but words failed me, caught in a moment that felt like an eternity.

The doppelganger took a step towards me and her empty eyes seemed to register my every emotion. »What would you do if you could change your past again?« she asked in a voice that was both demanding and challenging. The silence that followed was oppressive and I felt a storm brewing inside me. It was as if she was testing me to see if I was ready to accept the truth about myself – a truth that could be so painful and liberating at the same time.

As I searched my doppelganger's eyes, I felt the surroundings change. The bright light on the ceiling flickered irregularly and an ominous shadow crept across the floor. Without warning, the power went out in the entire corridor. Darkness enveloped me and the eerie encounter with my doppelganger was overshadowed by an abrupt loss of light.

The contours of the room blurred in the complete blackness and all sounds fell silent. My senses were overwhelmed by the sudden darkness and I felt panic rising inside me. The doppelganger's questions still echoed in my head, but her words were swallowed up by the oppressive blackness.

I groped for a foothold in the darkness, feeling cold wall surfaces under my fingertips that offered me no way out. The sudden silence was deafening and I lost my bearings in the darkness. The inexplicable power cut made me doubt reality for a moment – as if I were trapped in a nightmare from which there was no awakening.

CHAPTER 6

The light suddenly returned, as if someone had flicked the switch. In the darkness that had enveloped me, it gradually flickered, revealing a corridor that had changed in appearance. The once gleaming white surroundings now looked aged and slightly dilapidated. The walls were riddled with cracks, chipped layers of paint and fine layers of dust bore witness to the years that had passed without a trace. The floor creaked under my footsteps, as if it wanted to absorb every weight of time. It was as if the hallway had absorbed the traces of days gone by.

Every step seemed to confirm the new, weathered reality. The bright light that once made everything seem sterile and impersonal had turned into a dull, almost nostalgic glow. There were cobwebs hanging in the corners of the walls and a musty smell in some places that took my breath away. I could feel how the hallway had not only aged on the outside, but also exuded an oppressive weight of the past. Time seemed to have left its mark here, and every crack and crevice seemed to hold a secret.

Suddenly, the silence was broken by a rhythmic knocking. At first it was a soft thumping, hardly more than a faint heartbeat, echoing on the walls. But the knocking gradually became louder, more regular, almost as if someone was drumming on the brickwork with incessant beats. It was as if the hallway had begun to speak and was sending me a hidden signal. I stopped abruptly, listened intently and felt the knocking shake my core.

With trembling hands, I stepped closer to the wall where this strange sound seemed to be coming from.

The surface was rough and marked by the years. As I placed my fingers on it, I felt the vibrations that continued in a steady rhythm. It was as if the wall had its own heartbeat that was slowly getting louder. I could feel the beats echoing in my ears, giving me an uneasy feeling of trepidation. Each beat seemed to say more to me than words could.

Hesitantly, I raised my hand to return the sound, as if to enter into a silent dialog. My knocks echoed in the now aged silence of the hallway, and I listened to see if anything would change. The rhythmic tapping remained, and with each of my own taps, the intensity seemed to increase. The vibrations became clearer, as if they were waiting for an answer. I pressed my hand harder against the wall, trying to understand the mysterious rhythm that manifested itself like a silent command in the dilapidated walls.

At that moment, as I was absorbed in the interplay between the knocking and my own echo, a soft voice came to me from the depths of the wall. Its words were barely more than a whisper, but they were unmistakable: »You were not alone.« The voice sounded gentle, almost as if it was trying to comfort me, while at the same time revealing an unspoken truth. I stood paralyzed, unable to take my eyes off the dilapidated wall. The words reverberated inside me, and in the oppressive silence they seemed to permeate every corner of the hallway.

For a moment, time seemed to stand still. I felt the words echoing inside me and a quiet certainty grew within me, telling me that even in this deserted place there was no complete loneliness. Nevertheless, the voice remained enigmatic, as if it wanted to tell me something about my own past without showing me the exact path.

With a trembling voice, I asked, »Who are you?« My question hovered in the stuffy air as I approached the wall, as if I could find the answer in its cracks. But the wall didn't answer, it just kept tapping in an incessant beat that made me feel like I was trapped in a silent dialog. The words »You were not alone« still echoed in my head as I looked at the rough surface that now seemed so much more than masonry. It was an archive of past voices and unspoken memories.

I slowly withdrew my hand from the wall and took a step to the side as the knocking continued quietly. The atmosphere of the hallway had changed noticeably: The light that had returned now revealed every unevenness and every crevice reminiscent of times gone by. The hallway was no longer the immaculate, sterile space I had known before, but a place marked by the scars of time. It seemed as if every spot where paint had come loose told a story – stories of loneliness, loss and silent encounters that had become embedded in the walls.

As I walked on, I felt the rhythmic tapping intensify. It seemed as if the wall was incessantly setting a beat that led me further and further into this aged corridor. I forced myself not to take my eyes off the fragile details that showed me the way and concentrated on every single beat, which seemed to indicate that I had not been forgotten. The words of the voice – so clear and yet mysterious – seemed to whisper to me that there was something lurking in this place that reached beyond my presence.

With every step I took into the dilapidated hallway, I felt an invisible presence take hold of me. It was as if the walls seemed to know that I was searching for answers and were now pulling me into an inescapable web of past and present. The monotonous knocking that accompanied me seemed to be the only anchor in this strange reality. It gave me the feeling that someone – or something – was strangely close to me without me being able to see it.

Suddenly the knocking took on a new, more intense rhythm. I paused, my hand still trembling on the cool wall, when suddenly the familiar, gentle voice rang out again: »You weren't alone.« The words sounded more insistent now, almost demanding, and they seemed to get louder with every beat. It was as if the wall wanted to confirm to me once again that there was still a presence in this weathered hallway, amidst the cracks and faded paint – a presence that had never completely left me.

I felt my breath catch in my throat as the voice faded into a final, almost inaudible whisper. The rhythmic tapping continued, but subsided over the following seconds until it finally faded into an almost eerie silence. At that moment, everything stopped.

CHAPTER 7

As I continued down the corridor, I could still feel the leaden echoes of previous encounters. At that moment, my gaze fell on a door whose presence suddenly and inexplicably appeared amidst the faded brightness. The number 313 was emblazoned on the door in conspicuous numerals. I faltered and stared at the number as if it was recalling a long-forgotten memory without me knowing where it came from. The number was familiar to me, and yet I couldn't understand why it should appear here. A strange unease spread through me as I took a step closer to the door.

I touched the cool surface of the door with trembling hands. The years had left their mark: Scratches, peeling paint and a hint of rust were reminders of times gone by interwoven in this place. An inner urge to fathom the mystery of this apparition drove me forward. The figure seemed uncanny. My thoughts whirled and I could not detach myself from the strange presence of the number 313. It was as if the door was a portal to a lost world whose shadows still lived within me.

I carefully pushed down the door handle and the door slowly swung open. Behind it was a room that felt like an abandoned hospital room. The sterile coldness of the room was omnipresent, and the faint glow of a flickering light revealed the room in brittle detail. Nothing was alive except for a single bed that stood in the center of the room. The bed was surrounded by medical equipment that responded to flashing lights and soft sounds.

I entered and closed the door behind me. The room was filled with silence, interrupted only by the monotonous whirring of the medical equipment. My footsteps echoed on the smooth floor as I surveyed the room. Every corner seemed to bear witness to the abandoned past of a place that might once have been a haven for pain and healing. But now it was all just a ghostly shell of days gone by.

An old-fashioned monitor hung on the wall above the bed, its flickering light casting an eerie image. The display was faded, yet I could clearly make out my own name, accompanied by a simple heart-shaped line that seemed so flat it had lost all vibrancy. The letters appeared in clear, black numerals, without the usual spark usually associated with life and meaning. »What does that mean?« I whispered. The sight gave me pause, as if the machine was observing my existence with cold detachment.

I stopped and stared spellbound at the monitor. Was this evidence of a past self or a hint of something still lurking in the shadows of this place? The flat heart line that appeared under my name looked as if it had lost all pulse. My hands trembled and I wondered if I had gazed into an abyss that threatened to swallow me whole.

With a queasy feeling, I turned around and left the hospital room. But before I closed the door behind me, I stopped for a moment to look at the eerie image on the monitor one last time. The room seemed filled with the chill of times past, and every pixel of the flickering screen carried the weight of a silent message. I couldn't shake the feeling that this display was more than just a random relic, but a kind of reminder that resonated deep inside me.

When I re-entered the hallway, the atmosphere seemed to change again. The dilapidated state of the hallway, the aged walls and the dim light gave me the impression that time had stood still in this place. Every movement, every step seemed to be accompanied by an eerie premonition. I could feel an invisible veil over reality, blurring the boundaries between past and present.

Suddenly, I spotted another door at the end of the corridor that seemed eerily familiar. Its simple design, the faded sign and the fine cracks in the surface magically attracted me. I walked towards it, driven by a mixture of fear and curiosity that pulsed through me like an incessant current. As I stepped closer, I could see that the number 313 was once again emblazoned on the door – a sight that once again took my breath away. The repetition of this number sent my mind racing.

With a feeling that was somewhere between horror and unbridled curiosity, I pressed the door handle. The door creaked open, revealing a narrow corridor that led into the darkness of another room. I stepped inside and the flickering light revealed that it was an operating theater.

The sterile interior was filled with an oppressive emptiness and the room seemed abandoned, as if it had remained untouched for a long time. The walls, covered with faded wallpaper, bore witness to days gone by when life and pain went hand in hand here.

A brightly lit bed stood in the center of the room. Surrounded by medical equipment with silently flashing lights, it seemed to be the only witness to past operations. Next to the bed was a small table on which instruments lay. The room looked deserted. I move on.

CHAPTER 8

I discover a cupboard covered in dust. The floor creaked under my hesitant steps. I hesitantly opened the squeaky cupboard door and my gaze fell on a dusty tape recorder lying among yellowed clothes. The device, made of rusty metal, radiated an eerie coldness. I gingerly lifted it out, felt the cold breath of memory and wondered if this relic was once evidence of a lost life. My hands trembled.

My heart pounding, I sat down on the worn floor and pressed the button on the tape recorder. A faint crackling filled the silence before a voice reached me – my own voice, but strange and aged. The recording was rough, the words indistinct, but clear enough to shake me. »Guilt, loss and the moment in the hallway,« the voice proclaimed in a monotone, almost indifferent tone. Every sound seemed to hang heavy on my soul, as if the words had brought forth buried secrets. The words echoed in my mind, awakening memories I had thought long forgotten and casting doubt on the reality of my own existence.

The recording continued, and the voice took on an accusatory tone. »You failed when the moment came in the hallway,« she whispered as she continued to speak of guilt and loss. At that moment, a painful memory forced its way into my consciousness – a fragment from a dark night when a car accident turned my life into a nightmare. I remembered the deafening crash, the crashing of metal and glass, and the bright light that bathed the rain-soaked road in blood-red colors. The image of a lifeless body, motionless and abandoned, flashed in my mind and a cold shiver ran through me.

This memory, so fragmented and yet so vivid, became inextricably linked with the words of the recording. Each syllable seemed to draw me deeper into the abysses of my past, where guilt and loss lurked like shadows.

I closed my eyes and let the words of the recording penetrate me, while the memories of the car accident came back stronger and stronger. The pain of that night was indelible, and the image of the lifeless body on the rain-soaked road was burned into my memory. The voice continued to speak as if to reproach me with the burden of my own guilt. »You weren't strong enough,« it murmured, and in those few words there was an oppressive heaviness that crushed my heart. The moment in the hallway that the recording spoke of seemed to intertwine with the accident, as if both events were part of a larger, sinister plan. My thoughts swirled and I felt the darkness of the past threatening to overwhelm me as I tried to think clearly.

I rose slowly, clutching the old cupboard and the tape recorder tightly as if they could protect me from the approaching storm. The words of the recording echoed in my ears, and the pain of remembering was overwhelming. My thoughts were a chaotic jumble of guilt, loss and inexplicable grief. I wondered if the recording was a silent reproach to me or if it was meant to warn me. Every memory of the accident, of the broken glass, of the lifeless body, made the cold of the past rise up in me. The voice in the recording acted like a merciless judge, showing me my mistakes without offering me any possibility of redemption.

With trembling fingers, I gently placed the device back on the dusty floor and took a step back to process the recording in peace. The room around me seemed to change, as if the walls were feeling the weight of my memories. The pale light cast long shadows, and echoes of past deeds seemed to lie in every corner. I tried to form a clear thought, but the words of the recording and the image of the car accident blended into an opaque whole. »Guilt, loss and the moment in the hallway« – these words penetrated my consciousness as if they wanted to reveal the truth about my life so far. The eerie coldness that enveloped me was not only physical, but also an expression of the emotional emptiness that I had been carrying with me all these years.

When I finally tried to collect myself, I stood motionless and stared into the darkness of the deserted room. The recording had awakened something in me that I had long thought buried – a truth that was painful and unavoidable. The sharp, merciless look in the mirror of memory made me realize the cold reality of my fate. In that moment, as the last words of the recording faded into silence, all the memories merged into a single, unmistakable cry. I felt the guilt and loss envelop me, and the thought of the accident – of the lifeless body lying on the rain-soaked road – burned itself into my heart.

With one last look at the old tape recorder that bore silent witness to my past, I stood there, shaken inside and at the same time determined to accept the truth. The darkness around me seemed to gradually recede, but the scars of guilt and loss remained. Without further hesitation, I turned away and stepped out into the hallway, where the shadows of my memories lived on unceasingly. The weight of the past and the eerie presence of these places captivated me, while every step revealed to me the path and the mystery of my own existence, without mercy.

CHAPTER 9

The corridor branched out abruptly, as if it was constantly splitting into new directions. In front of me was a corridor immersed in the deepest, most impenetrable black. This blackish nothingness almost magically drew me in, as if invisible threads were pulling my soul under its spell. I stood hesitantly on the threshold of this dark path, my heart pounding restlessly. Without knowing what to expect, I stepped into the black corridor and immediately the darkness engulfed all light. Every step I took seemed to sink into absolute nothingness, but then fleeting images began to flash up on the cold walls.

At first, they were just shadowy shadows, barely more than fleeting outlines that passed by like ghosts on the walls. Suddenly the images became clearer and more intense. A car crash flashed before my eyes – a moment in which metal and glass shattered in a chaotic crash. The scene seemed as real as if I had been there and almost stopped my heart for a moment.

The image had barely died down when it switched to a shot of an abandoned hospital corridor. Sterile corridors, bare walls and the monotonous whirring of medical equipment characterized the scene, which seemed like a gloomy echo of days gone by. Shortly afterwards, another image flickered into view: a funeral. Mourning faces, a dark coffin and the cold breath of transience passed me by as the images changed in rapid succession.

The further I walked down the black corridor, the more intense the flickering scenes became. The images looked as if they were a collection of all the painful moments of my past – or perhaps the horrors of a world that had long since become alien to me. As these ominous fragments drifted past the walls, a familiar voice suddenly penetrated my inner self. It was my own voice, unmistakable and yet alien, whispering to me with firm clarity: »You didn't want to know.« The words echoed like a merciless reproach in the absolute blackness, and a cold shiver ran down my spine. I stopped abruptly, unable to detach myself from the images or the voice that echoed in my mind.

The flickering images became faster and faster, and the scenes seemed to merge in this maelstrom of accident, hospital and funeral. The sight of the shattering car was combined with the cold whirring of the machines and the mourning faces at the funeral. Each scene evoked memories in me that I would rather have forgotten. The thought of the lifeless body on the rain-soaked road left behind by the accident burned painfully into my consciousness. In the midst of this nightmarish kaleidoscope, the voice came to me again, this time more insistent and almost contemptuous: »You didn't want to know.« Its repetition was like a rebuke, a compelling reminder of my own past and all the secrets I had buried for so long.

With every step through the black corridor, the darkness seemed to get thicker. I felt how the cold and the eerie images made my heart heavy. The corridor seemed to want to show me the way to a truth that I had previously ignored out of fear of the pain. The images on the walls became more intense, and at every fleeting moment a new fragment flashed out – an accident, a hospital room, a silent funeral. It was as if the corridor had become an archive of my deepest guilt and loss. All the while, the voice that reproached me for my own failures kept penetrating my insides: »You didn't want to know.« These words sounded like an ominous rhythm that inevitably presented every memory to me.

I walked on, and the darkness seemed to transform into an eerie presence that cast a spell over me. The images now flickered so quickly that they almost merged into a single, painful moment. A car crash, the moment of impact, the scattered metal – all of this mingled with the images of an abandoned hospital room where the machines pulsed in a monotonous beat. At the same time, the dull shimmer of a funeral appeared, where the silent faces of the mourners seemed like mute witnesses to a past pain. These visual fragments made my heart tremble, and the burden of guilt seemed to grow heavier.

In the midst of this raging maelstrom of images and memories, the voice penetrated my inner self again, louder and more demanding than before. Her words resounded in the darkness, as if they were dropping all masks: »You didn't want to know.« These words seemed to take away any false hope, any possibility of repressing the pain. It was as if my entire existence was gripped by an inescapable judgment at that moment. I felt my thoughts constricting, every memory, every pain associated with guilt and loss becoming inescapable in that black corridor.

The corridor now seemed endless, and the flickering interplay of images and the eerie voice became an incessant stream that drew me into the depths of my own past. I could do nothing but lower my gaze and follow my steps, even though each step led me deeper into the abyss of my memories. The images intermingled in an ominous dance that felt like a mirror of my innermost fears. The visual cacophony of accidents, hospital corridors and funerals became a harrowing revelation of myself that I could no longer ignore.

When I finally reached the end of the black corridor, the darkness only gradually gave way to a diffuse, faint light. But the ominous images and the urgent voice lingered inside me. In this faint light, everything was so ghostly, as if reality was beginning to melt away. My senses were exhausted from the impressions and my heart was still pounding to the beat of the incessant repetition: »You didn't want to know.« These words gave me the feeling that I had arrived at a crossroads where the truth had torn down all my resistance.

Involuntarily, I paused as the images flashed before my eyes in a final, desperate flash. The car accident, the sterile hospital and the mournful funeral came together as a single moment in which all my guilt and loss came together. The voice that revealed this ominous truth to me echoed inside me – a constant reproach that held me in its shackles. »You didn't want to know,« she whispered again, and her words seemed to rob me of all resistance. For a moment, it seemed as if time paused, as if all the painful memories and the urgent voice merged into a single, unspeakable moment.

With a heavy heart and trembling legs, I left the black corridor and stepped back into the old, dilapidated hallway. There, in the dim light, everything seemed to take on its usual, albeit altered, shape. But the impressions of the corridor haunted me incessantly.

CHAPTER 10

I entered the gloomy archive room, where the pale light cast faint shadows over dusty shelves and yellowed files. The room smelled of old paper and mustiness, as if time was trapped in the dusty documents. In a secluded corner, I discovered an old, wooden cupboard whose doors creaked as I slowly opened them. Among numerous yellowed folders and files, a single patient file stood out – it had my name on it. My hands began to tremble as I carefully touched the thin, brittle paper. The name was written in clear but faded letters, etched into the pale material as if it was trying to tell me something unmistakable.

I slowly opened the file and my eyes glided over the soberly worded medical reports. Amidst the factual diagnoses and notes, one finding stood out in particular: »dissociative amnesia after traumatic event.« These words hit me with the force of an unexpected blow. A cold shiver ran down my spine as I read the clinical language that seemed to document my own fate. It was as if someone had meticulously recorded every aspect of my deepest memories – and my deepest forgetting. The diagnosis seemed at once disconcerting and undeniable, as if it were revealing to me the reason for my inner suffering.

My gaze continued to wander over the pages until I reached the edge, where a short note was emblazoned in fine handwriting. The words, carefully written in ink, read: »She must not see it.« This warning, so simple and yet so insistent, gave me pause. Who had written these words and what did they mean? The message seemed both familiar and strange to me, as if it concealed a dark secret that must never be allowed to come to light. At that moment, the file was a living witness to my hidden past, mercilessly revealing a truth that I had long tried to suppress.

With trembling fingers, I leafed through the pages again as the words of the diagnosis and the mysterious note echoed inside me. Every detail of the file – the dates, the names of the doctors, the examination findings – seemed eerily connected. The sober reports about my condition brought back memories of a fateful accident: the moment when everything broke and I lost my sense of self. The image of a lifeless body, lying motionless on the rain-soaked road, forced itself into my consciousness, accompanied by a feeling of infinite guilt and despair. This fragmentary memory, which I had suppressed for so long, now found its expression in the medical records.

The room around me seemed to get heavier, as if the file was carrying the weight of all those painful events. I closed the patient file slowly and my mind raced. The words »dissociative amnesia after traumatic event« penetrated deep inside me, while the mysterious handwriting on the back of the file gave me an ominous warning. The lines »She must not see« sounded like an unmistakable command, giving me the feeling that there were things that must never come to light – secrets that were too dangerous to be revealed.

Indecisive and at the same time driven by an undefined compulsion, I carefully placed the file on the old desk that stood in a dark corner of the room. The shelves around me were crammed with files that told of past fates and hidden tragedies. The pale light flickered uneasily and the shadows on the walls seemed to whisper stories long forgotten. In this haunting atmosphere, I realized that I was facing a part of myself that I had long repressed. The file was not just a document, but a silent witness to a period of my life, one of pain and loss.

I took a step back and breathed deeply as my heart pounded irregularly. The diagnosis hung heavy in the air and the ominous words from the back echoed in my head. Every breath seemed to carry the weight of my own history that I had forgotten for so long. The light in the room flickered as if to show me the way to some hidden knowledge, and the silence was broken only by the soft rustling of old papers. At that moment, I realized that I was at a crossroads: the truth of my own identity lay hidden in those yellowed pages, and no matter how hard I fought it, it would catch up with me.

Involuntarily, I turned away from the desk and walked slowly to one of the shelves to look for more clues. But my gaze kept returning to the patient file, which looked like a dark reflection of myself. The diagnosis – the words that documented my loss and the trauma of my accident – seemed to explain everything that I had been unable to understand in recent years. At the same time, there was this ominous note that made me feel like someone had warned me to stay away from this information. The words »She mustn't see it« were like an echo of past orders that wouldn't let go of me.

My thoughts were interrupted by a soft noise as the door to the archive room slammed shut behind me. For a brief moment, time seemed to stand still while the reality around me threatened to sink into darkness. I turned slowly and looked into the dark corridor that led out of the archive room. There, in the faint glow of a flickering light, everything seemed familiar and unreal at the same time. The eerie silence made my heart beat faster and I knew that I couldn't escape the truth – the truth that lay hidden in those files.

With trembling hands, I picked up the patient file again and reread the lines that documented my life in bitter detail. The matter-of-fact diagnosis and the forbidden note combined in my mind to form an indissoluble construct of guilt and memory. As I stroked the back with a trembling voice to feel the ominous words, I heard them clearly: »Don't let her see it.« This warning made me pause, while a feeling of powerlessness overcame me, as if a final, definitive command was echoing inside me.

The file lay heavy in my hand and its pale paper reflected the bitter truth of my past. Every letter, every line seemed to confront me relentlessly with a trauma that I could never fully overcome. My thoughts whirled as I gazed into the depths of my memory – into the abyss of what I had lost and what had remained forever alien to me. In that moment, I realized that I could no longer hide from the truth, as painful as it was. But the more I grasped, the more a dark secret was revealed that was beyond my control.

With heavy steps, I finally left the archive room and stepped out into the long, deserted corridor.

CHAPTER 11

Just as I crossed the threshold, I heard a soft noise behind me. I slowly turned around – and there he was. A man in an immaculate white doctor's coat. His face was half hidden in shadow and his eyes looked cold and distant, as if they had already scrutinized countless souls. He stood motionless, as if he had been suspended in time, and yet his presence seemed to awaken in me a long-forgotten feeling of trepidation.

In a voice that sounded at once soft and eerily vague, he began to speak without the slightest hint of haste in his words. »Subject,« he said in a tone that lacked any warmth, »you are in a simulation.« These words hit me like a blow and a cold shiver ran down my spine. The term »simulation« made my previous reality seem questionable – as if all the events I had lived through were just an artificially created state, an experiment in which I was involuntarily playing the leading role.

The man in the doctor's coat continued to speak as if to reveal a dark secret to me that was beyond the limits of my imagination. »Subject, everything you have experienced is part of a larger plan,« he continued, his voice calm and insistent. He explained in short, precise sentences that my memories, my pain and even my loss had not been accidental, but the result of a carefully orchestrated experiment. His words penetrated deep inside me and cast doubt on the authenticity of my entire existence. The cold, matter-of-fact tone made me feel that he felt neither sympathy nor empathy – he was merely the messenger of a truth that seemed both terrifying and irresistible.

I stood motionless, listening to every syllable of his statement reverberate in my mind. »Subject, you are part of this simulation,« he repeated in an almost monotonous rhythm as he scrutinized me with a penetrating gaze that seemed to reveal all my innermost fears. The idea that my whole life had not been real, but a mere construct, made my heart beat faster. Every memory, every painful moment that I had repressed for so long suddenly became visible in a new, eerie light.

Suddenly, in the midst of this surreal encounter, I felt something change in my field of vision. I could hardly believe what was happening: the man in the white coat began to flicker, as if his figure was unstable. A fleeting moment – and when I blinked – he was gone. In his place, a single stethoscope lay alone on the cold floor, shimmering dully in the diffuse light of the corridor. I knelt down, took the silent witness of that uncanny apparition in my hand and felt reality slip away from me in an instant.

The man's words still echoed inside me. »Subject, you are part of this simulation,« they echoed, and with them the incessant repetition of the message that everything I had thought was real was just part of a cruel experiment. The stethoscope in my hand was the only proof that the encounter couldn't have been a figment of my imagination. It was as if the cold metal construction was silently reassuring me that I was indeed not alone – that there were forces controlling and manipulating my life.

Confusion, fear and a pressing curiosity mingled within me as I slowly stood up again and walked down the deserted corridor. Every step seemed heavier now, as if the weight of the words and the realization that my existence was contrived weighed like lead on my soul. The eerie encounter with the doctor – or whatever he might have been – left me teetering on the edge between reality and illusion. I wondered if all the painful events I had experienced were really my own memories or if they were just staged fragments of a larger, incomprehensible simulation.

The hallway was shrouded in an eerie silence, broken only by the soft echo of my footsteps. As I walked on, I could feel my thoughts becoming entangled in an impenetrable web of doubt and fear. The stethoscope remained firmly in my hand as if to show me the way, but it offered no answer, only a silent reminder of what I had just experienced. The repeated salutation »subject« sounded like a promise that I could not escape – a promise that my life would never be the same, that it was now under the control of unseen forces.

I stopped for a moment to look at the empty corridor, where the darkness and the pale light battled with each other. The cold breath of loneliness enveloped me, and yet I felt a strange certainty that this encounter was only the beginning of something greater. The man's words and his sudden disappearance left me with an ominous emptiness that deepened with every heartbeat. The idea that my entire existence was merely a simulation became more and more pressing, while the reality around me turned into an opaque mosaic of memories and doubts.

Suddenly, the image of the man flashed in my mind again, his gaze, his cool voice – and then the ominous words he had left me. In an almost hypnotic state, in which every fiber of my being was tense, I repeated the sentence: »You are part of this simulation.« I closed my eyes as if to banish the sight of the mysterious doctor, and when I opened them again, all trace of him had disappeared. In his place lay only the stethoscope, silently sending me the message that the boundaries between truth and madness were more blurred than ever before.

With trembling hands and a pounding heart, I clutched the stethoscope tighter as I continued down the corridor. Every step was accompanied by the feeling that the world around me had changed – as if the fabric of reality had been torn in places. The doctor's words, his vague, eerie speech and the abrupt disappearance of his figure made it clear to me that I was trapped in a game whose rules I didn't understand. And yet a part of me remained trapped in the question of whether everything I had experienced was just a test – a test in which I could never escape as a »subject«.

As I paused in a moment of infinite silence and gazed deep into the darkness of the corridor, I was struck by a feeling that could hardly be put into words. It was as if time stood still at that moment and allowed me to take in all the impressions . The soft echo of my footsteps, the cold metal of the stethoscope in my hand and the eerie words that reverberated like an echo in my mind created an image that I could never forget. With one last, uncertain glance into the emptiness of the corridor, I took another step.

CHAPTER 12

All around me, whispering voices, strange and yet familiar, reached my ears. It was as if voices from times gone by lingered in this corridor. There was a steady murmur in the air, a fleeting sound that mingled with my breath. The words came softly in an indefinable rhythm that made me feel like I was trapped in a dream. Nevertheless, I could hear fragments that stuck in my mind like splinters.

In the midst of this tapestry of sound, individual words emerged, clear and insistent enough to give me a shock. »Guilt«, it sounded, and this word carried an oppressive weight. This was followed shortly afterwards by the word »truth«, the meaning of which gave me an oppressive feeling. Then I heard, almost whispering and reproachful, »it was you«. These words echoed inside me, as if they were reproaches for past deeds that I could not escape.

The voices seemed to fill every corner of the hallway as I walked along. The eerie melody of the voices enveloped me like an invisible veil, and every step in the cold hallway seemed to draw me deeper into this enigmatic mystery. I could never really escape.

The whispering voices seemed to intensify as I moved deeper into the hallway. There was a hint of despair in their fleeting sounds and I heard them settle in my thoughts. Between the indefinable murmurings, individual words crystallized, reverberating in me like cutting reproaches. »Guilt« sounded once, as if the voice was accusing me directly, and the sound of this one syllable gave me pause. The word »truth« followed shortly afterwards, spoken with a coldness that made my blood run cold. Then, in an almost whispering tone, »it was you« was heard, as if it were a personal accusation. These words sounded repeatedly and incessantly, a steady stream of memories and accusations that spread through my insides.

It was as if the voices formed a melody of their own, uniting to form an ominous mantra. Every sound seemed to penetrate deep into my soul and open up old wounds that I had long tried to hide. The words echoed in the endless expanse of the hallway, as if they were forcing me to confront my past. Their eerie repetition penetrated my consciousness like a painful reproach, ever present.

Suddenly my eye fell on an old shelf. Curiosity spurred me on and I approached it with hesitant steps. I discovered a video cassette on the shelf. The label on it was barely legible, but with a little light I recognized the words: »Last attempt«. A cold shiver ran down my spine as I held the old tape in my hands.

Looking at the cassette brought back memories of hidden secrets and long-suppressed moments. I sensed that there was more to this relic than first met the eye. I hesitantly stroked the label while an eerie anticipation grew inside me. Every fiber of my being urged me to learn more about the origin of this latest attempt. The coldness of the tape and the eerie light of the hallway merged into a moment that made me realize the boundaries between past and present, immediately.

I sensed that this cassette had not landed here by chance. I hesitantly approached an old video machine that was standing in a secluded corner. The thought of playing the tape filled me with hope and fear at the same time. Memories and premonitions battled inside me, lining up like shadows. The hallway seemed to come alive at that moment, as if it was pulling me towards it with invisible hands.

Every step I took reinforced the feeling that the past was inexorably closing in on me. The faint crackle of old technology and the dull hum of equipment punctuated the moment I decided to unravel the mystery. A sense of foreboding permeated every fiber of my being as I walked hesitantly along. I faltered, unable to take the next step.

With the video cassette in my hand, I stood motionless in the dim light of the hallway. The whispering voices had softened by now, as if retreating into the darkness, but their ominous words – »guilt«, »truth«, »it was you« – still echoed in my mind. It was as if the label »last attempt« was a final appeal to my subconscious to remind me of the inescapable reality.

I knew I didn't have an easy choice, because every decision led me further into the labyrinth of my own memories. With a queasy feeling in my chest, I lifted the tape, ready to explore its contents.

CHAPTER 13

I sat down in front of the old video recorder and pressed the play button. The flickering image appeared and I saw myself – behind the wheel of a worn-out car. My face was streaked with tears and my eyes, in a state of painful emptiness, gazed silently into nothingness. I was driving on a rain-soaked road, the rain pattering incessantly against the windshield, and every wipe of the windshield seemed to reveal a reflection of my inner despair.

Then the picture changed abruptly. I lost control in a fraction of a second. The camera recorded everything in painful detail – how the car skidded, tires squealed, and a violent impact threw the world into chaos. The car crashed into a hard object and the occupants were thrown in all directions. I saw how the car lay deformed and disfigured on the road after the impact. At that moment, time seemed to stand still and the fleeting moment of total collapse left an unbearable void.

When the image reappeared, it showed a different scene inside the vehicle. Sitting next to me was another person whose facial expression and posture precluded anything of life and hope. This person lay motionless as blood ran slowly over the broken upholstery. The contrast between the crying me behind the wheel and the lifeless passenger was overwhelming. It was unmistakable that this person was dead – a silent witness to a terrible event that had taken place in a single, cruel moment. The sight made me tremble inside, and a dull feeling of guilt pressed heavily on my heart.

As the video continued, the images became blurred and the scenes changed in an eerie rhythm. Suddenly a voice rang out – my own voice, which was clearly audible in the recording. With firm, almost cold-sounding clarity, it whispered: »What will you do when you know?« These words sounded like an ominous reproach that held all the shadows of the past. It was as if the recording was not only showing me the accident, the loss and the pain, but also asking me if I was ready to accept the truth about my own existence. The question made me freeze as the image slowly faded to black and the video ended abruptly.

I sat there, staring at the now blank screen and felt an icy chill spread through me. The recording had sucked me into a vortex of memories, guilt and unspoken fear. The words echoed in my mind as I tried to get a clear thought. Had all of this been just a distorted dream, a coincidental montage of events, or was there something deeper behind it? The thought that my entire life could be part of a larger, incomprehensible experiment made me shiver.

I put the remote control aside with trembling hands. The image of the accident, the lifeless person and my own tears, which were captured in the recording, were indelibly etched in my memory. Every second of the video seemed to convey a message that simultaneously reproached me and gave me the feeling of being trapped in a simulation from which there was no escape. The question that was asked at the end gnawed at me like a piercing pain.

I remembered the words of the whispering voices in the hallway that had accused me of knowing more than I wanted to admit. Those voices had already burned individual words like »guilt«, »truth« and »it was you« into my consciousness. Now that I saw myself in that video – crying, driving and then witnessing a fatal accident – it all seemed connected. Part of me wanted to deny the truth, but the painful evidence was laid bare before my eyes. The recording acted as a mute judge, pointing out my own failings while paving the way to a painful realization.

The image faded, and the flickering light of the old monitor left me in a state between memory and loss of reality. I could feel the ominous murmur inside me, merging with the recording. The question: »What will you do when you know?« hovered in the air and forced its way inexorably into my consciousness. It was like a cry from the darkness, telling me that I had to face my destiny – no matter how painful it might be.

I stood up, my eyes still wet from the tears I had shed during the recording. The room around me was cold and empty, and the low hum of the electronics echoed like a distant heartbeat. The recording seemed to be not only a relic of a past accident, but also a signpost to a dark future in which the question of guilt and truth left no room for chance. The car accident, the loss of a loved one and the ominous words merged into a picture that sent me plunging into the abyss of my own memory.

I didn't know if I would ever be able to process these realizations or if they would haunt me forever. The camera had captured it all – the agony, the despair and the guilt that dwelled within me. At that moment, it seemed clear to me that I could no longer hide from the truth, even if that truth would plunge me into a state of unimaginable darkness. The video had given me a glimpse into a reflection of myself that I would have loved to forget, and yet it was now inescapable to me.

With every fiber of my being, I felt the urge to answer the question, but the fear of the consequences paralyzed me. The fleeting glimpse of the broken picture showing the accident and the eerie silence after the last question left me stuck in a time warp of pain and guilt. I stood there, caught between the painful memory of the accident and the eerie question that took my breath away: »What will you do when you know?

At that moment, a feeling swept through me as if the world around me was changing, as if the boundaries between reality and fiction were finally dissolving. The video that had so painfully confronted me with my own past was now more than just a recording – it was an inescapable mirror in which all my hidden fears and failings were revealed. My thoughts circled incessantly and I felt the coldness of realization settling into me.

I reached for the device as if I wanted to play it again, perhaps to find a new clue, but the moment I raised my hand, the image died for good.

CHAPTER 14

I walked on. Suddenly, at the end of a side corridor, I discovered a door that stood out from all the others. It was open and a warm, almost heavenly light was coming from inside. Behind the door, there was a peaceful atmosphere that contrasted sharply with the gloomy gray of the rest of the hallway. The bright light seemed to draw me in, as if to offer me a sanctuary, free from the oppressive memories and endless reproaches that had haunted me for so long.

I slowly approached the open door, and every step I took seemed to change the space around me. The cool, bleak atmosphere of the hallway gradually gave way to an almost reassuring warmth in the bright room behind the door. The walls were painted in soft, friendly colors, and a soft, soothing hum filled the air. It was as if this room was a sanctuary where the torments of the past faded into the background for a moment. There was an air of peace in the silence and I paused for a moment, feeling a faint sense of hope welling up inside me, although doubt and fear still nagged at my mind.

With trembling steps, I entered the brightly lit room. As soon as I had crossed the threshold, I suddenly heard a gentle whisper that crept right inside me. It was like the voice of a child, gentle yet insistent, and it seemed to come from the shadows of the room behind me. The words, barely audible, penetrated my mind: »If you leave, it will come back.« The sound of this warning gave me pause, for its meaning was at once strange and familiar. It was as if someone – or something – was telling me that any escape from this place would only reignite the incessant cycle of pain.

I stood still and listened while the soft whisper echoed inside me. The child's voice had a tone that sounded innocent and at the same time held a grim warning. It was as if these words came directly from my own past – a part of memories that I had long buried. The sound of the voice mingled with the soft rustle of the curtains blowing in the gentle breeze, creating a feeling as if time had paused at that moment.

The last door now lay before me, brightly lit and inviting, while the rest of the corridor remained in oppressive darkness. The peaceful aura of the room behind the door seemed to offer me a way out of the endless shadows, a refuge where I could finally find peace. But inside me stirred the ominous reproach of the childish voice that had whispered in my ear: »If you leave, it will come back.« Those words were like an echo, assuring me that leaving this place would only continue the cycle of disaster. It was as if the decision to go this way would also mark the beginning of a new, relentless nightmare.

At this crucial moment, I felt my heart tighten. I had to choose: Should I walk through the peaceful door, follow the warm light and try to make a fresh start, or should I return to the gloomy hallway where all the oppressive voices and shadows were waiting for me?

The choice seemed like a fine line between redemption and further decline. Every breath felt as if it weighed on me the weight of my own guilt and lost time. The soft glow behind the door lured me in with the promise of peace and oblivion, while the hallway in front of me held the endless, unchanging.

The light behind the door seemed to give me comfort, while the dark hallway reminded me of the inevitable cost of my past. It was as if I was at a crossroads.

With a trembling hand, I placed my finger on the cool door handle. For a moment, time seemed to stand still as the soft call of the child's voice and the gentle glow of the light merged in an eerie unison. In that moment, I felt all my fears and hopes come together in a single, fragile instant. The decision lay before me – the possibility of entering the bright room and perhaps finding a way out of the endless cycle of pain, or returning to the dark hallway where the shadows of the past never quite disappeared.

I closed my eyes briefly to let the urgent words sink in and then opened them again, my gaze fixed on the brightly lit room. The warm glow behind the door seemed like a promise, as if it was telling me that something new was beginning here, something that could leave the torments of the past behind. At the same time, however, the ominous warning of the childish voice that had whispered in my ear penetrated inside me and filled me with the dark premonition that nothing could ever be over for good.

At that moment, as I touched the handle and hesitantly took a step towards the bright room, I was struck by an intense feeling of fear and doubt. I knew I had to make a choice – either enter this peaceful, light-filled room or return to the dark, endless hallway where the voices and shadows continued to incessantly dictate my fate. The choice lay before me like an invisible pact, a pact between the promise of redemption and the inevitable return to the dark memories.

With one last deep breath that seemed to give me courage, I didn't lower my gaze. I stopped on the threshold, my heart hammering in my chest as the moment seemed to stretch out. The silence was almost palpable, and the child's soft whisper, sounding repetitive, echoed in my ears: »If you leave, he'll come back.« These words were like a fateful command, making it clear to me that any decision I made now would have inevitable consequences.

The room behind the door continued to shine with a peaceful, almost comforting light that promised me a way out of the shadows of the past. But the dark corridor in front of me, with all its endless memories, also cast a spell over me. At that moment, when all my questions and fears culminated in a single, painful moment, the world seemed to stand still. The decision was mine to make, and I knew with every fiber of my being that this moment would decide my fate.

As I stood at the threshold, my hands trembled and my heart beat in an irregular rhythm. I didn't know whether I would ever find the strength to enter the room behind the door or whether I would return to the dark corridor to face the shadows of my past. In this moment of infinite tension, between light and darkness, between hope and despair, the choice seemed to tear my whole existence into the abyss or offer me a way out.

Then – without me being able to think any further about my decision – the moment broke.

CHAPTER 15

I realized that the hallway was more than a mere corridor – it was a place between life and truth, an in-between realm where reality and memory were inextricably interwoven. While the friendly lights of the room flickered softly behind me, I felt the shadows of the corridor welcoming me with open arms. The cold, endless corridor, filled with the voices of times past, offered me the opportunity to face my own memories. I knew that anything was possible in this hallway – both redemption and pain. The hallway challenged me to look at myself as I really was, and made me realize that there was no way out but to dwell in my own truth.

In this quiet moment, all my memories came flooding back. The images I had suppressed for so long flooded inexorably into my consciousness. I saw the painful moment of a car accident that shattered everything and the loss that followed. Every moment, every scene was imbued with an intense guilt that I could never quite shake off. The memories of those dark hours – the desperate drive, the silent weeping and the incomprehensible failure – mingled with the bitter realization that I had never really forgotten all these events.

The burden of guilt weighed heavily on my heart and the loss of those who were close to me became deeply rooted inside me. It was as if the hallway was absorbing all the pieces of my life and revealing to me the unvarnished truth of my existence. I felt how all the shards of my past came together to form a picture that confronted me bluntly and without equivocation.

The eerie whispering voices that had previously echoed through the corridors had now become quieter, but their message remained in my ears. In every fleeting sound, in every breath of darkness, there were words that reminded me of the inescapable reality: guilt, truth, failure. These words hovered in the air like invisible reminders, pulling me deeper into the maelstrom of my memories. I could literally feel the reproaches as if they were coming from the cold walls of the hallway. The room seemed to whisper to me that I could not hide from what I had been and that repressing the past could never lead to redemption. Every memory that rose up in me challenged me to acknowledge my own mistakes and accept the pain, painful as it was.

As I walked slowly through the hallway, the environment around me seemed to change. The rusty walls and the pale light became silent witnesses to my inner turmoil. With every step I took, the lost images of my past returned – like an unstoppable stream that could not be stopped.

I remembered the cold, rainy nights when I sat at the wheel and felt the end of my world. The pain of the accident, the moment when life seemed to lose its meaning, forced itself into my memory. The guilt I felt was no longer just a fleeting thought, but an oppressive shadow that accompanied my every move.

The decision to stay in the hallway was not an easy one. There were moments when the enticing glow of the bright room behind the open door tempted me to start again, but deep down I knew that the hallway was a place where I had to face the truth and confront my own memories. The hallway had become a mirror that showed me all the painful moments I had tried to suppress for so long. I knew there was no way out but to escape the constant confrontation with my past. Every breath filled me with the certainty that I could no longer ignore my guilt and my loss.

In the twilight of the hallway, where the pale light penetrated in weak rays through the cracks in the dilapidated walls, I felt the weight of the years and the echo of all those who had been lost here. The surroundings seemed alive, as if the corridor held the secrets of all. With each step, a new memory returned, pulling me deeper into the abyss of my own past. I remembered the painful nights, the moment of the accident when life lost its luster, and the reproaches that followed like a dark shadow. Each memory was like a blow that reminded me that there was no escape, only a constant return to the truth.

With every step I took, I felt my mind open up and the memories spread inexorably through me. The guilt and grief were no longer just faint hints, but became an all-encompassing part of my existence. Every breath revealed to me the bitter truth that I could no longer hide from myself. The hallway was an endless space that forced me to embrace all my fears and guilt because it was the only way I could face reality.

As I stopped in the middle of the corridor, I felt all my memories return in their full force. Shame, pain and guilt came together in a single moment that hit me relentlessly. The echo of past words urged me to accept my own truth. I realized that I could no longer hide from myself. In that moment, the relentless realization that there was no way out embraced me. The hallway doesn't end as long as you refuse to see yourself.

Printed in Great Britain
by Amazon

62290806R00037